Orla
the Inventor
Fairy

Join the **Rainbow Magic Reading Challenge!**

Read the story and collect your fairy points to climb the

To Daphne, who loves rabbits and purple

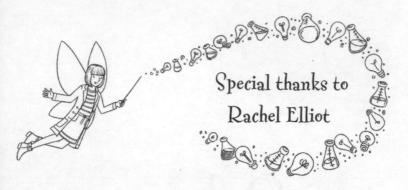

Special thanks to
Rachel Elliot

ORCHARD BOOKS

First published in Great Britain in 2019 by The Watts Publishing Group

1 3 5 7 9 10 8 6 4 2

© 2019 Rainbow Magic Limited.
© 2019 HIT Entertainment Limited.
Illustrations © Orchard Books 2019

HiT entertainment

A CIP catalogue record for this book is available from the British Library.

ISBN 978 1 40835 514 5

Printed and bound in Great Britain by CPI Group (UK) Ltd, Croydon, CR0 4YY

MIX
Paper from
responsible sources
FSC® C104740

FSC
www.fsc.org

The paper and board used in this book are made from wood from responsible sources

Orchard Books
An imprint of Hachette Children's Group
Part of The Watts Publishing Group Limited
Carmelite House, 50 Victoria Embankment, London EC4Y 0DZ

An Hachette UK Company
www.hachette.co.uk
www.hachettechildrens.co.uk

Orla
the Inventor
Fairy

By Daisy Meadows

ORCHARD

www.rainbowmagicbooks.co.uk

Jack Frost's Spell

Those brainy fairies make me cross.
One day Jack Frost will be their boss.
I'll solve each baffling mystery
And make each great discovery.

I'll steal their magic books away
And grow more crafty every day.
No clever-clogs in history
Will be as brilliant as me!

Contents

Chapter One
The Gallery of Inventions

"Wow, look, Rachel," Kirsty Tate said to her best friend. "These cameras are more than one hundred years old."

"Wow!" agreed Rachel Walker. "I love photography."

The best friends were inside the Science Museum's Gallery of Inventions, looking

at a display about cameras. They were
at the Science Museum for a very special
sleepover. Hundreds of families and
groups of friends had come to camp
inside the museum for one night. Rachel
and Kirsty had come with Mr Tate,
Kirsty's dad.

So far, it had been even more exciting
than they had expected. Their visit to the
planetarium had turned into a magical
adventure in Fairyland. The girls had
met the Discovery Fairies – Aisha the
Astronaut Fairy, Orla the Inventor Fairy,
Annie the Detective Fairy and Elsie
the Engineer Fairy. They were all very
worried because Jack Frost had broken
into Mission Control and stolen their
magical notebooks.

"I can't wait to find out what the next

activity will be," said Rachel.

"Me too," said Kirsty. "But I keep thinking about the Discovery Fairies. Without their magical notebooks, they can't help to inspire people who make amazing discoveries or invent things like these cameras."

"We've already helped them to get one of the notebooks back," said Rachel. "I'm sure that soon we'll get the chance to help find the others."

Just then, a man in a bow tie clapped his hands to get everyone's attention. The boys, girls and parents gathered around him.

"Welcome to the Gallery of Inventions," he said. "My name is Professor Aldous Fidget. From the wheel to the computer, the world has been made a better place

by imaginative inventors who had a
dream and made it come true. So, what's
your dream?"

"A flying car," shouted out a little girl.

"A time machine!" called a little boy.

"A self-watering flowerpot," said
another girl.

"All excellent ideas," said Professor
Fidget, clapping his hands. "We have a
great activity for you. We would like you
to become inventors for the evening. On
the tables in the middle of the gallery are
all sorts of inspiring things. There are also
tablets for you to work on. We can't wait
to see what you make."

"I know exactly what I want to
invent," said Kirsty. "After our adventures
with Cara the Coding Fairy, I've been
practising coding at home. Let's invent a

friendship quiz on the tablet."

"That's a great idea," said Rachel.

They sat down next to a younger girl
called Daphne. Her eyes were shining
with excitement as she typed lines of
code into the tablet.

"Are you coding too?" she asked. "I'm
going to make a purple rabbit that hops

across the screen."

"We're making a quiz," said Rachel.

The gallery was filled with an excited buzz. The children were working hard, and the parents were sitting at the side of the room, sipping tea and chatting. Professor Fidget strolled around, talking to the inventors and looking at their work.

"Yes, it's working," said Daphne after a short while. "Look."

She pressed start and a smiling purple rabbit hopped across the bottom of her screen. It stopped, waved a paw, and then hopped away again.

"Daphne, that's brilliant," said Rachel. "Show us again."

The rabbit hopped on to the screen again. But this time it was grey and hopped upside down. It looked unhappy.

"What's gone wrong?" cried Daphne, tapping the screen. "This isn't what I wrote."

Across the gallery, a boy suddenly flung his tablet to the ground and stamped his foot.

"Why won't it work?" he cried.

There was a sudden commotion among the parents. A little robot was tying all their shoelaces into knots.

"I'm sorry," sniffed the girl who had invented the robot. "It's supposed to fasten shoelaces, not tangle them."

Rachel and Kirsty stood up and looked around. Every invention was going wrong. All the children looked confused and upset.

"I bet this is happening because Orla the Inventor Fairy doesn't have her magical notebook," said Kirsty.

Just then, there was a shout from the far end of the gallery.

"It works!" said a loud voice.

The girls followed the other children and the professor. They were gathering

around a thin boy with a cap
pulled low over his face. His pyjamas
were decorated with lightning bolts and
he had a scarf wrapped high around his
neck and chin. On a table in front of
him was a small, blue ball with a white
button on top.

"Show us what it can do," said

Professor Fidget.

The boy pressed the white button.

"Slug breath!" shouted the blue ball.

The boy sniggered and pressed the button again.

"Banana brain!" the blue ball yelled.

"Good heavens," said Professor Fidget.

"Nincompoop! Blockhead! Pesky pain!" The boy pressed the button again and again.

"That's enough," said the professor, frowning. "What a shame that the only invention that's working is so unpleasant." The boy who had invented it stuck

out his tongue and blew a raspberry at
the professor. There were gasps from the
parents around the room.

"Kirsty, I don't think that's a boy at all,"
Rachel whispered. "No child would be so
rude and mean. I think it's a goblin."

Chapter Two
Fairyproof!

"My insulting machine is the best invention in the world," the boy yelled at the professor.

He turned a dial on the side of the blue ball and pressed it again.

"Stinky socks!" shouted the ball, louder than ever. "Slime for brains!"

"See the orange notebook on his table?" said Kirsty suddenly. "It reminds me of Aisha's magical notebook."

"Wait," said Rachel. "Look at his hands. They're blue!"

"And I can see a spiky beard, even though he's trying to hide it with his scarf," added Kirsty. "He's Jack Frost!"

Daphne came to stand beside them.

"That boy's got the only invention that's working," she said.

"I don't think he's done it all by himself," said Kirsty, looking at the magical notebook.

Professor Fidget was shaking his head.

"I can't approve of such a rude and unkind invention," he said.

"You're all silly and boring," Jack Frost snapped. "I'm off."

He grabbed the notebook and ran out of the gallery. Everyone started talking at once. In the muddle, Rachel and Kirsty hurried out of the gallery too. Jack Frost was standing in the corridor, pulling off his pyjamas.

"Stop!" Kirsty shouted.

Jack Frost looked up and gawped at them.

"You two?" he exclaimed. "You pests are always following me around. Leave me alone."

"Not until you give back the notebooks you stole," said Rachel.

Jack Frost flung the pyjamas and cap on the floor. His cloak swirled around him and his beard and hair looked spikier than ever.

"Fine," he snapped. "I'll go somewhere you can't follow me, you bothersome humans."

He raised his wand.

"Rachel," Kirsty cried. "Lockets!"

The girls fumbled to open the lockets they both wore. Each had a pinch of fairy dust inside. As the dust sprinkled down on them, Jack Frost waved his wand.

"Hold on to his cloak," Rachel exclaimed. "We can follow him."

There was a bright flash of blue light.

Then the cloak yanked the girls forwards.

Rachel and Kirsty tumbled into a snow
bank. They sat up, shaking snow from
their hair and wings. They were on the
ground outside the Ice Castle.

"We're fairies," Kirsty realised.

"You're a pain in the neck," Jack Frost snarled. "But I'll stop you."

He raised his wand and shot an ice bolt at them. At once, they felt their wings stiffen with cold. Ice crackled all over them, freezing their arms and legs. It even froze their hair.

"I can't move," said Kirsty in a panic.

"Me neither!" said Rachel.

"Good," said Jack Frost. "You can stay here and watch me go into my castle, with my notebook. And when I'm inside, none of the other fairies will get their notebooks back either.

I've invented a spell to stop fairies from coming in. It's called Fairyproof, and it recognises fairies even if they're magically disguised. Ha!"

He strode towards the castle with the notebook under his arm.

"We have to get free of this ice," said Kirsty. "Look, Jack Frost is almost at the castle."

"If he gets inside, we'll never get the notebook back," said Rachel.

They tried to wriggle and

break free from the ice.

"My arms and legs feel as if they've been turned into stone," said Kirsty. "Thank goodness we can still talk."

They watched as Jack Frost reached the entrance and turned to look at them. He waved and then skipped into the castle.

"Oh no," groaned Rachel. "What are we going to do?"

Chapter Three
The Wooden Goblin

"I can hear something," said Kirsty. "It's getting louder."

Silvery voices were calling their names from above. A moment later, three of the Discovery Fairies fluttered down in front of them.

"Oh, you poor things," exclaimed Orla,

waving her wand.

The ice melted away and Rachel and Kirsty could move again.

"Thank goodness we found you," said Annie. "Queen Titania saw that you had arrived in Fairyland and sent a message to us at Mission Control."

"We came to find you straight away," added Elsie. "Aisha stayed to look after Mission Control."

"What are you doing here?" Orla asked.

Quickly, Rachel and Kirsty explained what had happened at the Science Museum. When Orla heard about the notebook, she let out a squeak of excitement.

"The orange notebook is mine," she said. "But how am I going to get it back

now that Jack Frost has the Fairyproof spell? I have to stay here and find a way into the castle."

"I'm sorry, I can't stay with you," said Elsie, looking worried. "I have to get back to help Aisha at Mission Control."

"And I must go to the palace to tell the

queen what's happened," said Annie.

"We'll stay and help Orla," said Rachel at once.

Gratefully, Elsie and Annie hugged them goodbye and zoomed away. Orla smiled at Rachel and Kirsty.

"Thank you for staying to help," she said. "But I don't know what to do next. How can we get inside a castle that will recognise any magical disguise?"

"Maybe we need a disguise that isn't magical," said Kirsty.

"But we can't make ourselves look like goblins without magic," said Rachel. "And I'm sure Jack Frost will have told the guards to suspect anyone who's not a goblin."

"Perhaps we don't need to change the way we look at all," said Orla.

She suddenly sounded excited. Tucking
her short, black bob
behind her ears, she
pulled a notepad
and a pencil out
of her white lab
coat. As she started
scribbling notes and
sketching diagrams,
Rachel and Kirsty
exchanged a curious
glance.

"She must be
inventing something,"
said Rachel. "I can't
wait to find out what it is."

After a few moments, Orla smiled and
slipped her notepad and pencil back into
her pocket.

"I have a plan," she said. "Have you heard the old human legend of the wooden horse of Troy?"

Rachel and Kirsty nodded.

"I read it at school," said Rachel. "Greek soldiers got inside a guarded castle by hiding inside a huge wooden horse."

"Yes," said Orla, "and that's exactly how we're going to get inside the Ice Castle. Watch this."

She raised her wand, and a huge wooden goblin appeared in front of them.

"It's a giant," said Rachel. "But how is it going to help us get into the Ice Castle?"

"Follow me," said Orla.

She flew up to the top of the giant wooden goblin. With a tap of her wand a

trapdoor opened in the goblin's head.

"Oh, it's just like the wooden horse of Troy," said Kirsty. "If we hide inside, the goblins won't see us."

"And it won't be a magical disguise, so the Fairyproof spell won't stop us," added Rachel.

"I'm going to use magic to put the giant goblin outside the castle entrance," said Orla with a smile.

"We should hang a note around its neck," said Kirsty. "The goblins have to think it's a present."

With a flick of Orla's wand, a sign appeared around the goblin's neck.

Dear Goblins,
This is a present to say thanks. You're the best!
From a friend

"Let's hide inside," said Orla. "Then I'll transport us to the castle gates."

Chapter Four
Searching the Castle

The fairies huddled together inside the head of the wooden giant. They heard the gates open. Then there was the sound of goblins squawking and chattering.

"I put the giant on wheels so it's easy to pull inside," Orla whispered.

"Fingers crossed," said Rachel.

The wooden giant lurched forward.
Kirsty flew over to peep out of one of the
giant's eyes.

"It's worked," she said. "We're going in."

The wheels of the giant squeaked as
they rolled into the castle courtyard.

"Who's it from?" asked one of the
goblins.

"Let's get Jack Frost," yelled another.
"He'll want to see this."

"They're all running into the castle,"
said Kirsty.

As soon as the last goblin left the
courtyard, Orla lifted the trapdoor. The
three fairies flew out and hid behind a
nearby pillar.

A few seconds later, the goblins came
back with Jack Frost. He paced up and
down in front of the giant. Then he

stopped and glared at the sign around its neck.

"Who would give you a present?" he asked. "And what are they thanking you for? It must be a mistake. I'm sure it's meant for me."

The goblins started squabbling and
Rachel took Orla's hand.

"Hopefully they will all stay here and
argue for a while," she said. "Meanwhile,
we can go looking for the notebook.
Come on, I know the way to the throne
room."

They slipped into the nearest corridor
and zoomed deep into the castle. The
walls were wet with damp, and mouldy
icicles hung from the ceiling.

The throne room door was open, and Kirsty bravely peeped inside.

"It's empty," she said. "He's hidden that orange notebook somewhere in the castle. Let's start searching."

They flew around the throne room, peeping into every nook and cranny. Rachel dived under the throne and Orla shook out the dusty curtains. Kirsty checked through piles of empty sweet wrappers and broken plates. She found five issues of *Ice!* magazine and three lost woodlice, but no notebooks.

"Let's look in Jack Frost's bedroom," said Kirsty. "I think I remember the way."

Jack Frost's room had changed since the last time they were there. The bed was decorated with pictures of Jack Frost's face. The curtains had the word 'Frost' printed all over them in silver. Even the rug was in the shape of Jack Frost.

"Check everywhere," said Rachel.

The fairies checked under the mattress and inside the wardrobe. They found boxes of feather boas and swirling cloaks, but no notebooks.

"We have to think," said Rachel. "Where else could it be?"

"Looking for this?" said a voice.

The fairies whirled around. Jack Frost was standing in the doorway, holding the orange notebook in his hand. He glared at them.

"I don't know how you got past my amazing Fairyproof spell," he snapped. "But you are never getting this notebook back."

Rachel and Kirsty held hands. They could feel each other trembling. How were they going to escape?

"Why do you want the notebook?" Rachel asked.

"It's going to make me famous," said Jack Frost, stroking his spiky hair. "I'll be the only one to make discoveries. Everyone will know my name."

"The best inventors don't care about being famous," said Orla in a gentle voice. "They care about making the world a better place. But they won't be able to invent anything if you don't give my magical notebook back."

"Rubbish," Jack Frost scoffed.

"It's true," said Kirsty. "Inventors and engineers have changed the world. They don't care about everyone knowing their name."

"Then they're nitwits," Jack Frost replied, tucking the notebook loosely under his arm. "With this, I can do anything I want."

The fairies exchanged worried glances.

"What do you want to do?" asked Orla.

"None of your business," said Jack Frost. "Thanks to my new notebook, I've invented a spell that will banish you from Fairyland for ever. Then I can do whatever I like."

Orla turned to Rachel and Kirsty. Her eyes sparkled.

"I have an idea," she whispered. "He can't cast that spell on us if he can't see us."

As Jack Frost took a deep breath, Orla waved her wand. Instantly, all three fairies vanished.

Chapter Five
Invisible Fairies

Jack Frost blinked and rubbed his eyes.

"Where did you go?" he growled, stepping into the room. "An invisibility spell? I want it!"

Rachel and Kirsty were still holding hands.

"I've got an idea," Rachel whispered

into Kirsty's ear. "He's not holding the notebook tightly. Maybe we can take it out from under his arm."

"What about Orla?" said Kirsty. "We can't leave without her."

"If we get the notebook, she'll see it flying through the air," said Rachel. "She'll follow us."

They fluttered their wings and rose up until their feet were just off the floor. It was hard to fly when they couldn't see themselves.

"I'll get you," Jack Frost said, reaching out his spare hand in front of him.

He almost touched Kirsty's wing. She edged around behind him, holding on to Rachel's hand. They didn't even dare to whisper. Together, they reached out to the notebook. It slipped easily out from under Jack Frost's arm.

"He hasn't noticed," whispered Rachel.

They fluttered backwards as Jack Frost

looked down and gave a yell of fury.

"Fly," shouted Kirsty as she sped away with the book. "Orla, follow us."

She zoomed down winding steps. Jack Frost came pounding along behind her.

"I'm right beside you," panted Rachel. "We must fly faster – he's catching up!"

The fairies zipped in and out of rooms and up and down stairs. Jack Frost was wheezing and holding his sides, but he didn't stop.

"Give me back my notebook!" he shouted.

"Rachel, which way is out?" Kirsty cried.

Just then, Rachel spotted the corridor that led to the courtyard.

"You're not going to escape," shrieked Jack Frost. "Guards! Goblins!"

"We can't leave without Orla," said Rachel. "But we can hide."

Pulling her best friend along, she flew out into the courtyard and up to the head of the wooden goblin. Below, a crowd of goblin guards squawked in surprise. All the girls could see was the orange notebook rising up in the air.

"Catch them, you numbskulls," Jack Frost bellowed.

"Catch who?" one of them replied. "It's a floating book."

"It's being carried by invisible fairies," Jack Frost yelled at him. "Now get them!"

The goblins started jumping up, clutching at the air with their bony fingers.

"I don't like the sound of invisible fairies," one of them wailed.

Rachel and Kirsty reached the top of the wooden goblin and dropped inside through the trapdoor.

"Oh my goodness," said Kirsty, sinking to the floor. "I have never flown as fast as that."

"Me neither," said Rachel. "It's so strange not being able to see you."

"Let's look out through the eye holes and see what Jack Frost is doing," said Kirsty.

Down in the courtyard, Jack Frost was hopping with rage. He had a crowd of goblin guards around him.

"Listen to me, you useless lot," he yelled. "There are invisible fairies inside that stupid giant goblin. They've got my orange notebook, and I want it back. So climb up to that trapdoor and get them out."

"Oh no," said Kirsty in alarm. "What are we going to do? And where is Orla?"

"We have to think of a way to stop them from getting in," said Rachel. "We could bolt the trapdoor shut."

"But then Orla wouldn't be able to get in," said Kirsty.

The roars and squawks of the goblins were getting louder.

"I think they're climbing the legs," said Rachel. "How long are we going to be able to stay in here?"

At that moment, the wooden giant tilted sideways a little. Rachel slid to the left and Kirsty had to cling to the eye hole to stay still. Outside, the goblins squealed and ran.

"Oh my goodness, how is this happening?" cried Kirsty. "It's walking!"

Chapter Six
Mission Control

Rachel pulled herself up to the other eye hole.

"It's walking towards the way out," she said.

The goblins were in a panic. Rachel and Kirsty even saw some of them trying to climb the castle walls.

"Stop that thing," Jack Frost yelled. "It's

just a bit of wood shaped like you."

He started to stride towards the wooden giant. Then he saw a crowd of goblins running towards him.

"Stop!" he screeched.

The goblins kept running.

"They're not stopping," said Rachel, gasping.

The Ice Lord turned and ran from the

crowd of frightened goblins, still yelling. The giant ducked to go through the entrance, and then Rachel and Kirsty were outside the castle.

"Hurray!" they cheered.

As soon as they were out of sight of the castle, the giant goblin stopped. Rachel reached out to squeeze Kirsty's invisible hand.

"What do we do now?" she asked.

At that moment, the trapdoor opened. Rachel and Kirsty looked up and saw a wand floating in the air. It swished, and there was a puff of fairy dust. Then Orla appeared, holding the wand.

"I can see you," said Kirsty in relief. "Oh, and I can see myself again too. Thank goodness!"

"It was so strange to look down and

not see my own legs," said Rachel with a laugh.

"How did you know where we were?" asked Kirsty.

"I saw the book float into the wooden goblin," said Orla. "I just had to think of a way to get us all out safely."

Smiling, Kirsty flew up through the trapdoor and gave Orla the notebook.

"Thank you," said Orla. "We made a great team today. We actually invented a way to defeat Jack Frost."

"That really is a wonderful invention," said Rachel, laughing.

"Will you come to Mission Control with me?" Orla asked. "I can't wait to

return my notebook to the Discovery
Library."

"We'd love to," said Kirsty. "Let's go. I
don't want to be here when Jack Frost
finds the wooden goblin."

Orla led them away from Jack Frost's
icy corner of Fairyland. Soon they saw
the glass dome of Mission Control. It was
glittering in the sunshine. The entrance

panel slid open and the fairies flew inside.

"Welcome back," called three happy voices.

Aisha, Elsie and Annie darted towards them, smiling to see the orange notebook.

"Another of our magical objects is back where it belongs," sad Aisha.

"All thanks to Rachel and Kirsty," said Orla. "I couldn't have done it without them.

"Mission Control is busier than the last time we were here," said Kirsty, looking around.

When Jack Frost had taken the four notebooks, the computers and control panels had shut down. Nothing had worked. Now some of the buttons and screens were glowing, and there was a faint crackle from the live link to the International Space Station.

Orla fluttered into the Discovery Library and replaced her notebook on the shelf. There was a distant tinkling sound, and an orange glow filled the library. At once, even more computer screens lit up. Orla clapped her hands.

"Half of Mission Control is working again," she said.

All the Discovery Fairies were smiling, but Rachel noticed that Annie and Elsie still had sadness in their eyes.

"I promise that we'll help find your notebooks too," she said. "Jack Frost won't get away with this."

"Thank you," said Annie and Elsie, hugging them both.

"For now, I think I should send you back to your sleepover," said Orla.

"Before you do, could you refill our

lockets?" Kirsty asked. "Queen Titania lets us carry just enough fairy dust for one trip to Fairyland."

"Of course," said Orla.

She tapped the lockets with her wand, and silvery fairy dust streamed into the lockets. They shut with a click.

"Thank you," said Rachel.

Orla waved her wand, and Mission Control disappeared with a pop. Rachel and Kirsty were once more standing in the corridor outside the Gallery of Inventions. Their wings had disappeared, and they were human once again.

"We're back at the Science Museum," said Kirsty. "But this time Jack Frost isn't here."

As usual, time had stood still in the human world while the girls had been in

Fairyland. They peeped into the gallery and smiled. Things looked very different now. Everyone was smiling and talking. Professor Fidget was hurrying from table to table, commenting on the different inventions. Every single one was working perfectly.

"May I have your attention, please?" said the professor.

The girls slipped back into the gallery as people stopped talking to listen.

"Every invention I've seen here today is absolutely splendid," the professor said. "I'm pleased that this is not a competition, because I wouldn't want to have to choose between all these wonderful ideas. However, I would like to mention one name. Daphne is the youngest inventor here, and she has done an excellent job creating her purple rabbit animation. It just goes to show that you are never too young to make discoveries and dream up inventions. Please give yourselves a huge round of applause."

Everyone clapped and the girls went to join Daphne.

"Well done," said Rachel, smiling.

"Thanks," said Daphne. "I want to be an inventor when I grow up."

"Then I bet you will," said Kirsty.

"It's almost time for bed," said Professor Fidget. "But first, there are copies of some of the most famous toys ever invented in the middle of the room. I thought you might like to try them out."

Smiling, Daphne led the way towards a collection of spinning tops. Behind her,

Rachel and Kirsty shared a thoughtful glance.

"Jack Frost still has two of the magical notebooks," said Rachel. "I hope we can help to find them all."

"We can, and we will," said Kirsty. "Oh, I've just realised that we never finished our friendship quiz."

Rachel squeezed her hand.

"We don't need a friendship quiz," she said. "We already know that we're the best friends ever!"

The End

Now it's time for Kirsty and
Rachel to help ...

Annie the Detective Fairy

Read on for a sneak peek ...

SNUFFLE! SNORE! The Science
Museum echoed with sleepy noises. It
was the night of the big sleepover, and
every gallery was filled with mums, dads,
children and sleeping bags.

In the Discover Space gallery, only two
children were still awake.

"I'm too excited to sleep," whispered
Rachel Walker.

"Me too," said her best friend, Kirsty
Tate. "After our magical adventures
earlier, I keep expecting another fairy to
pop up."

The girls were lying next to each

other. There was just enough light in the gallery for them to exchange a happy smile. They loved sharing the wonderful secret that they were friends with the fairies.

"It's great that we helped Aisha and Orla find their magical notebooks," Rachel went on. "But Jack Frost still has the other two notebooks. Until we get them back, the Discovery Fairies won't be able to help, inspire or guide anyone."

Kirsty turned on to her side and propped herself up on her elbow.

"I'm sure we'll get the chance to help Annie and Elsie soon," she said.

The Ice Lord Jack Frost and his naughty goblins had been causing trouble again. They had stolen the magical notebooks that belonged to the Discovery

Fairies. Rachel and Kirsty had visited
Mission Control in Fairyland, where the
Discovery Fairies watched over humans
and fairies. Without their notebooks, they
weren't able to do their jobs.

"Shall we go for a walk around the
museum?" Rachel suggested. "It might
tire us out enough to be able to sleep."

"Great idea," said Kirsty. "We can
choose which gallery we want to visit
tomorrow."

Rachel took a couple of apples out of
her rucksack.

"Midnight feast," she said, grinning.
"Come on."

The girls picked up their torches and
tiptoed past the rows of sleeping people.
They left the gallery and came to a flight
of stone steps going down.

"I don't remember seeing those steps on

the museum map," said Kirsty. "I wonder what's down there."

"Let's find out," said Rachel.

They shone their torches down the steps and Rachel led the way. The air got colder.

Read **Annie the Detective Fairy** to find out what adventures are in store for Kirsty and Rachel!

Calling all parents, carers and teachers!
The Rainbow Magic fairies are here to help
your child enter the magical world of reading.
Whatever reading stage they are at, there's
a Rainbow Magic book for everyone!
Here is Lydia the Reading Fairy's guide to
supporting your child's journey at all levels.

Starting Out
Our Rainbow Magic Beginner Readers are perfect for first-time readers who are just beginning to develop reading skills and confidence. Approved by teachers, they contain a full range of educational levelling, as well as lively full-colour illustrations.

1

Developing Readers
Rainbow Magic Early Readers contain longer stories and wider vocabulary for building stamina and growing confidence. These are adaptations of our most popular Rainbow Magic stories, specially developed for younger readers in conjunction with an Early Years reading consultant, with full-colour illustrations.

2

Going Solo
The Rainbow Magic chapter books – a mixture of series and one-off specials – contain accessible writing to encourage your child to venture into reading independently. These highly collectible and much-loved magical stories inspire a love of reading to last a lifetime.

3

www.rainbowmagicbooks.co.uk

"Rainbow Magic got my daughter reading chapter books. Great sparkly covers, cute fairies and traditional stories full of magic that she found impossible to put down" - Mother of Edie (6 years)

"Florence LOVES the Rainbow Magic books. She really enjoys reading now" - Mother of Florence (6 years)

The Rainbow Magic
Reading Challenge

Well done, fairy friend – you have completed the book!
This book was worth 5 points.

See how far you have climbed on the
Reading Rainbow opposite.

The more books you read, the more points you will get,
and the closer you will be to becoming a Fairy Princess!

How to get your Reading Rainbow
1. Cut out the coin below
2. Go to the Rainbow Magic website
3. Download and print out your poster
4. Add your coin and climb up the Reading Rainbow!

There's all this and lots more at
www.rainbowmagicbooks.co.uk

You'll find activities, competitions, stories, a special
newsletter and complete profiles of all the
Rainbow Magic fairies. Find a fairy with your name!